Jackie's Gift

Julia A. Royston

Illustrations by Derrick Thomas

BK Royston Publishing LLC

P. O. Box 4321

Jeffersonville, IN 47131

http://www.bkroystonpublishing.com

bkroystonpublishing@gmail.com

502.802.5385

Cover Design: Derrick Thomas

Illustrations: Derrick Thomas

Book Layout: BK Royston Publishing LLC

ISBN-13: 9781689180115

Printed in the USA

Dedication

This is dedicated to every child that has a gift. It's in you.

You are Gifted.

Acknowledgement

I thank my Lord and Savior Jesus Christ for giving me another opportunity to write and entrusted this gift to me. Lord, bless the people who will purchase, read and pass along some of the knowledge located in this book.

To my husband, Brian K. Royston, the love of my life for loving and cheering me on so much that I can be and do all that God has placed in me. You are the wind, air, breath and engine beneath my wings. I love you...

To my Mom, my greatest supporter and best friend. To my Dad, who is in heaven, that I know is proud of me and always encouraged me to go for it. Thanks to all of the rest of my family for their love and support. A special thank you to Rev. and Mrs. Claude R. Royston for their love and support.

Thank you to Derrick Thomas who did another excellent job illustrating this book.

To every child who ever thought they were ordinary. There is a gift in you and I want you to use it.

Julia A. Royston

ntroduction

'rom birth, I had a lot of issues in my body. My feet were turned left to right when I was born so my mother turned my feet inward during every diaper change. Thank you mama. wore corrective shoes most of my life. I was always heavier than other girls and veighed one hundred pounds at six years old. I had a speech impediment until I was ight years old. I started wearing glasses at eight years old.

Vhen I turned nine years old, I participated in my junior choir at my church. I was hosen to lead a song and the rest, as they say, is history. With all of my ailments, I was ifted to sing. I took voice lessons to develop my skills and knowledge as a singer but nusic is my first love and gift. Over time, I have discovered and developed other gifts, alents and abilities that I utilize in my businesses to this day. Fortunately, I was raised by parents who recognized, supported and made sure that my gifts were financed. Through ny years of teaching in public schools, private schools and other public events, I have ince learned that I was extremely blessed to have parents like mine because there are nany children in the world who are not as fortunate.

Every child may not sing or have a musical gift, but everyone has been given a gift. Help a hild discover, develop and display that gift today. If you need me, reach out at ttp://www.juliaroyston.net or follow me on social media. Let's go!

'hank you.

ulia Royston

Meet Jackie Green!

She has a mother, June, a father, Jesse, Sr. and a brother named Jesse, Jr. or JJ for short. When Jackie was born, she had a lot of issues. Her feet stuck out sideways. She had trouble with her hearing from too much wax. She had trouble speaking because her tongue always got in the way. She had trouble with her eyes because she couldn't see very far so she had to wear glasses.

Jackie is loving, fun and has lots of friends in spite of her troubles at birth. One thing Jackie loved was music. Everyday Jackie would go down in the basement of her parent's house and listen to music over and over and over again.

One day, when JJ came in from soccer practice, he passed the basement door and heard Jackie downstairs singing. He opened the door, sat on a step out of sight and listened.

GET READY TO SHINE!
TALENT SHOW
OUR
STAR?

When Jackie went to school, she was good in all of her classes but wasn't good in sports. She was always picked last. Jackie didn't care she would just smile, giggle and have fun. Her teacher, Mrs. Camp would always say, “Do your best Jackie and have fun!”

One day when Jackie’s class was coming out of the cafeteria, Ms. Smith, the school counselor, was putting up a big poster. The poster read, “Talent Show” Next Friday in the Cafeteria. Sign-ups start tomorrow.

“Check in with your teacher, Jackie,” Ms. Smith said.
Jackie smiled back, but didn’t mention anything to her friends .

TALENT SHOW
ARE YOU OUR NEXT STAR?
GET READY TO SHINE!
ALENT
OW
ARE YOU OUR NEXT STAR?

At the end of the school day, Ms. Camp passed out the flyer that was a smaller version of the poster that Ms. Smith posted outside of the cafeteria.

It said the same thing, “Talent Show.”

Jackie reluctantly held up her hand to receive one and quickly put it in her backpack.

GET READY TO SHINE!
TALENT SHOW
ARE YOU OUR NEXT STAR?

When she got home, she put her backpack at the door, grabbed a snack and went downstairs immediately to practice. When mother got home, Jackie showed them all the smaller flyer for the Talent Show.

“I got the flyer for the talent show. Do you think I should participate?”

“Do you want to participate?” mother asked.

“I want to, but I don’t really think that I’m good enough for that yet,” Jackie said.

“Yes, you are. I’ve been listening,” JJ said.

“I agree. I’ve heard you downstairs too.” said mother.

“I agree too. From what I’ve heard, you sound wonderful,” said father.

“That’s it! Jackie should be in the Talent Show at school,” mother said.

The big day finally arrived. Jackie boarded the school bus with her cute dress, glasses to match, socks and Sunday shoes on.

"You look nice Jackie," the bus driver, Mr. Jones said before closing the bus door.

"Thank you, Mr. Jones," Jackie said as she went to her seat. Jackie rode the bus very nervous and worried about the Talent Show.

The entire school filled the cafeteria. When it was Jackie's turn, she opened the curtain and looked out into the audience to see her mother, father and brother, JJ to support and cheer her on.

Jackie became even more nervous but she knew she was ready.

Ms. Smith handed the microphone to Jackie and said quietly, “You ready?”

Jackie smiled and gave Ms. Smith the thumbs up. Ms. Smith walked off the stage and gave Harvey the sign to start the music.

The music started and Jackie opened her mouth and right on cue, sang the song perfectly.

When Jackie finished, all of the students and adults including her family stood and clapped for her performance.

Ms. Smith took the microphone from Jackie when she finished and said, “Wow, Jackie’s got a real gift.”

At the end of the program, other adults came up to Jackie’s parents to congratulate them on Jackie’s performance.

Even Mrs. King, the music teacher, congratulated Jackie and her parents and said, “I am going to have to pay more attention to Jackie and give her a solo in the upcoming pageant. She truly does have a gift.”

ICE CREAM
ALL FLAVORS
VANILLA
PEACH
COOKIE DOUGH
STRAWBERRY
PECAN
CHOCOLATE
MINT
CHERRY
GRAPE
PUMKIN

After Jackie’s performance, the Green family went to their favorite pizza place.

Mr. Green turned to Jackie and said, “Alright we’ve had a great pizza so that mother didn’t have to cook. What does my very gifted daughter want for a treat today?”

“A double dip of ice cream, chocolate and chocolate chip!”

“Ice cream it is,” father said.

“Yes!” said mother.

“Yippee!” said JJ as they dived their spoons into their ice cream dishes with huge smiles and happy hearts.

Thank you so much for reading Jackie's Gift by Julia A. Royston and illustrated by Derrick Thomas.

If your school or library would like to order more copies of Jackie's Gift, please reach out to:

BK Royston Publishing,

P. O. Box 4321,

Jeffersonville, IN 47131

5028025385

bkroystonpublishing@gmail.com

BK Royston Publishing sponsors fundraising Book Fairs for schools, non-profit organizations and other community events. For more information,

visit http://www.bkroystonbookfair.com

Thank you so much for reading Jackie's Gift. We know what Jackie's gift is but what is your gift?

Review Questions?

What was Jackie's last name?

How many brothers does Jackie have?

What sport does Jackie's brother's play?

What is one thing that Jackie is not good at?

What does Jackie do on the stage during the Talent Show?

Discussion Question

What is one thing that you enjoy doing?

What is your gift?

Vocabulary

Gift	Music	Performance	Sing
Stage	Solo	School	Talent Show

This is your stage below. What will you do as a performance on this stage?

Name____

Made in the USA
Middletown, DE
07 June 2021